THE GHOST DETECTORS

A HAYWARD HALL SHORT STORY

ALEXANDRIA BLAELOCK

BlueMere Books
MELBOURNE, AUSTRALIA

For permission requests, please contact
enquiries@bluemerebooks.com.

Ordering Information:
Discounts are available on quantity purchases. For details, contact orders@bluemerebooks.com.

The Ghost Detectors/Alexandria Blaelock
paperback ISBN: 978-1-925749-60-1
digital ISBN: 978-1-925749-61-8

Book Layout © BookDesignTemplates.com

THE GHOST DETECTORS

Zoo yawned and sighed to loosen his jaw as he looked through the spear tipped wrought iron gates, up at the house beyond.

He felt the kind of frisson that suggested the shoot was going to be a good one.

He turned and walked past the gates to the edge of the property, continuing his vocal warm up exercises by humming up and down a couple of octaves.

When the property was built, it had been situated in close to 30 hectares of gardens. But since the tragic events of 1905, it had been sold off little, by little, until all that remained was a monstrous house in an inappropriately small garden.

One of the gates hung drunkenly from a crumbling brick pillar, and he wondered how he could incorporate that into the show.

He pulled a stainless-steel straw from his pocket, put it in his mouth, and hummed up and down his vocal range.

As he looked up at the two-story house, he pulled a bottle of water from his bullet harness inspired tool belt and hummed a few bars of his favourite song down the straw and into the water.

Set the drone to rush down through the gates, over the overgrown drive and up to the wreckage of the portico?

He dropped the straw into the bottle and buzzed his lips, making them vibrate.

Nah, too hackneyed.

He walked back to the other side of the property, rolling his tongue, saying rrrrr up and down hid range, trying a very little to expand it.

From the outside, it looked exactly like what you'd would expect of a haunted house.

The land sales had resulted in the front door facing a street that was no longer there.

The side door, once with views over the croquet lawn, had become the de facto front door.

Consequently, the house had the appearance of turning away from you, though Zoo couldn't tell whether it was ashamed of what it had become, or whether it thought he was beneath its notice.

He was a man for whom all things are either black or white - no shades of grey.He liked straight lines and order; each of his avenues of interest were neatly compartmentalised away from all the others.

It was what made him so good at hosting *The Ghost Detectors* show.

Despite being the kind of person who would go into a stranger's home and straighten the pictures.

Though the fans loved it - home owners freaking out on camera, and he would coolly adjust the hang of a picture. It was almost his signature move.

Though of course, he didn't believe any of it. All mass hysteria.

The "new" drive up to the house bisected the lawn, enough off centre to make him uncomfortable

The garden, if you could call it that, was overgrown. Full-height trees and bushes had taken over the lawn so comprehensively that it would only be impossible to mow the grass on your hands and knees, blade by blade.

He flexed his jaw, yawning with his mouth closed.

The fountain on his left had once featured a woman in ancient draperies pouring water from an urn on her shoulder, but a lightning strike had split the statue in half and melted the fountain mechanism.

Or so the story went.

He pulled back to the side of the street, singing eeeee as he worked his way up two octaves, and ohhhhh as he sang down again. Once more trying a very little to increase his range.

The walls of the house remained at two stories, with a tower reaching a third on his right. The roof had caved in across several rooms, probably about the same time the portico collapsed.

Zoo stood, hands on hips, singing ooooo like a demented siren as he looked through the gate.

The yellow bricks were still clearly visible against the red, the diamond patterns still discernible through the dirt.

For a moment he thought he saw a woman silhouetted in a second story window, then realised it was sun glare.

Zoo sang his scales again, and only then permitted himself to drink some water.

Then he checked his tool harness for the necessities; torch, walkie talkie, notebook and pen, his phone, a Polaroid camera, voice recorder, his electromagnetic field detector, thermal camera, the Kinect camera, spirit box, ghost box, and motion detector.

Even though Brian, tech and comedic relief guy, had already checked them.

Pulling each device out of the harness, turning it on, checking the power, and putting it back again.

Camera operator Steve was taking background shots of the gates, house, and garden, while Josh set up the fixed camera feed to the laptop.

They had both daylight and night vision, focused on the house exterior. The cameras would record the team entering and exiting the building, along with any other phenomenon.

Brian was checking the portable cameras Steve and Josh would be using to film inside the house.

"Ready?" Zoo asked the team.

The men replied in the affirmative.

They walked across to where the midnight blue sports utility vehicle branded with *The Ghost Detectors* decal was backed up just inside the gates.

Steve started filming the introduction that would play before the title sequence, and while they walked across the lawn.

Zoo talked through the history as he spread the floor plans out on the bonnet.

"Mr Dewitt Fox, made his fortune selling goods in the Victorian Goldfields, and built Hayward Hall in 1868 with the proceeds.

"This house has seen many deaths, starting with Dewitt and ending with the suicide of Lucy Chalmers just five years ago.

"It's also seen the mysterious disappearances of two women named Morag Clementine, one in 1905, and one in 2030, and Henry Fox in 1922.

"The most haunted rooms are reputed to be the library," he pulled the ground floor plan to the top and pointed out the library.

"And the master bedroom," he pulled the ground floor plan aside to reveal the second story, and indicated that room.

"Reported phenomenon include hearing footsteps running up and down the stairs located here," he tapped the stairs on both floor plans, doors opening and closing themselves, objects falling from shelves, and of course, temperature changes."

Zoo looked around the group, "any questions?"

Brian asked, "How do you open the door to a haunted house?"

Josh rolled his eyes and replied, "with a skeleton key."

The all groaned while Zoo folded the floor plans and tucked them in his tool belt.

Steve waited a moment, and then said, "clear."

They regrouped just inside the focus of the fixed cameras, and Josh turned them on.

Zoo stood in the middle as the "star" of the show.

They waited for a moment, then Zoo called the crew together, "all right then, let's get this show on the road."

He rubbed his hands together, holding one each out to Steve and Josh as they walked into frame. Brian joined hands with Steve and Josh on the other side, careful to keep Zoo framed in the centre.

Zoo prayed out loud, "gods and goddesses of life, please protect us as we venture into the realm of the dead, and bring us safely out again.

"Gods and goddesses of the dead, let us pass through your realm safely and unharmed. And if your subjects are here in this place, please let us speak with them and hear their stories, and when we leave, keep only those who are yours.

"So be it."

And the men echoed him, "so be it."

"All right then," Zoo said to camera as the team backed up to fan around him, "it's sunset and we're here at Hayward Hall, possibly the most haunted house in Melbourne. As always, we go in live, and you get to come with us."

They turned their backs to the camera, and Zoo looked back over his shoulder, "are you ready?

"Then let's go!"

They walked, or perhaps more correctly waded across the garden towards the house.

As they got close, Steve and Josh pulled out the cameras and started filming.

Zoo and Brian waited until filming had started, then turned their tool belt equipment on, took their EMF detectors out and pointed them here and there as if trying to get a mobile phone signal.

"All fine so far," Zoo said, and Brian nodded.

Zoo climbed over a pile of rubble and up to the door, taking the key from his pocket and opening the door. It opened smoothly, and they walked inside.

"If you're wondering why the house is fairly well maintained," he told Steve and the audience, "Henry Fox set up a trust in 1908 to maintain the house. It remained intact until 2025 when Lucy Chalmers became the trustee, dissolved the trust, and used the funds to pay for her lavish lifestyle."

They walked through the door, across a small alcove and into a larger room.

"This area was originally the drawing room, and the library is just across the corridor."

The camera men panned across the room, highlighting the dust and peeling wallpaper, the sheet music still resting on the piano, the spotted mirror above the fireplace.

It was hard to know whether the ceiling had originally been painted, or whether the mould growth had made its own design.

Brian suppressed a scream, and Josh filmed his face. He shrugged, "I thought I saw someone," he said.

Zoo held his EMF detector up to show Steve he had two bars lit up. He tucked it back in his belt, pulled out the Polaroid, and took a picture in Brian's direction.

"With all this stuff still in here, it's hard to know whether you're looking at something paranormal or not."

Brian rubbed his temples, "this place is giving me a headache."

"Let's go across to the library," Zoo said, and Brian nodded.

Part of the library's ceiling had fallen down, leaving the beams exposed, and dislodging some of the books as it fell.

A long red hued wood table was stacked with books, almost as if someone had popped out of the room for just a moment, and would be back any minute.

Steve panned across the room, taking it all in.

"Wait," cried Zoo, "did you hear that?"

Brian nodded, "it sounded like a woman talking."

They looked wildly around the room, until a shelf crashed to the floor at the opposite end of the room, and they spun to look. Clouds of dust had flow into the air, and the cloud boiled as if someone was fanning the air.

Zoo got out his Kinect camera, and they saw a stick figure waving its hand, as if to clear the dust.

"We've got contact," he said, moving the device side to side to see what else was there.

And addressing the ghost, "Who are you? Why are you here?"

The dust cloud swirled, and the Kinect camera went blank.

He moved in back and forth in wider arcs each time, but the camera stayed blank.

Brian grunted and wrapped his arms around him, "I felt something brush by me."

Zoo headed toward the door they'd come in, and it started closing.

He caught the door before it shut fully, and felt it resisting his efforts to open it back up.

"Brian, give us a hand?"

He jogged over and together they managed to pry it back.

Zoo turned the corner, and heard something run up the stairs.

A mostly broken stained glass window shone blood-coloured fragments of light on the fuzzy strings of cobweb hanging from the banisters and moulding on the ceiling.

It was likely there was carpet underneath all the dust, but it was indistinguishable from the indeterminate pattern of the wallpaper.

"Did you hear that?" he looked at Brian.

"Sounded like someone walking up stairs."

Brian took his thermal camera from his tool belt and held it up to the landing, "cold spot on the landing.

"Moving upstairs."

Zoo paused to let them film the stairwell, then walked up the stairs, testing each tread fully before trusting it with his weight.

The rest of the team followed.

The door to the Master Suite was opposite the stairway, and when they got up the stairs, the door swung open invitingly.

The roof of the master suite had partly caved in, and grass was growing on the bed. The rest of the furniture around the walls was covered in dust, but appeared sound.

Zoo opened a drawer in the dressing table, "look, there's still clothes in the dresser." He paused for Steve to film it, then shut the drawer without touching them.

They looked at the top of the dresser, "some kind of green perfume bottle, compact, lipstick. Looks like they left in a hurry."

Despite the filth, the cheerful, sunny curtains, were perfectly still against the smashed windows.

"Try the Spirit Box?" asked Zoo.

Brian nodded, and pulled it out of his belt

Zoo asked again, "who are you? Why are you here?"

Static burst from the box, "Henry," followed by more static.

"Are you Henry Fox?" asked Zoo.

"Henry."

"What happened to you?"

"Where's Henry?"

Zoo frowned at the camera, "if this isn't Henry, then perhaps it's Morag Clementine, who'd been married just a few hours before she mysteriously disappeared.

"The police investigation at the time was inconclusive; no evidence of kidnapping, and no evidence of theft. The Detective in charge, an Inspector Morrison, noted his opinion that she'd absconded in the file."

"Talk to us Morag," begged Brian.

"Henry."

"Did Henry kill you?" he asked

"Henry.

"What happened to Henry?" Zoo demanded.

"Help.

"Scared."

Zoo and Brian looked at each other, then Zoo moved onto look at a picture of a young couple on a beach somewhere.

He couldn't help himself from straightening the picture, and his teamed smiled at each other.

Then it fell down.

They felt the atmosphere change and stiffened.

Zoo picked it up and tried to rehang it, but it slipped from his hands and fell a little further away.

He took a step forward, reached to pick it up, and fell through the floor face first to the sitting room below.

He lay stunned for moment, the dust half choking him, then asked, "Brian, are you there?"

There was no reply, and he struggled to turn over.

As the dust cleared, he saw a woman and a dog looking down through the hole at him.

"Careful," he said, "the floor isn't safe."

"No kidding," she replied.

"Wait, you're not real."

"Under ordinary circumstances I would be offended by that comment, but you're probably right."

"Who are you?

"Morag Clementine. I mean Fox."

Zoo cautiously sat up, "Am I dead or what?"

"Why are you asking me?"

"Aren't you a ghost?"

"I don't know, what's the date?"

"The date? What does that have to do with anything."

"Hold on a second, I'm coming down."

As he struggled to his feet, he heard her clattering down the stairs, followed by the dog.

She was wearing an old-fashioned dress, "you're the 1905 Morag Clementine?"

"1905?"

"Well, you can't be the 1905 disappearance and the 2030 as well."

"Why not?"

"Well, surely the original would be dead by the time the 2030 version was born."

"Ah, I see. You're assuming they're different people. Follow me."

She walked out of the drawing room, dog trotting behind and ducked behind the stairs.

He followed her out the door, and stood transfixed by the sunlight shining through the unbroken stained glass. He could fully appreciate the vibrant reds and greens of the twisted vine pattern.

The roof had a kind of moulded plaster leaf pattern which solved the Drawing Room ceiling mystery. The carpet was clean, with a discernible paisley pattern repeated on the walls.

Just moments ago, he'd seen it covered in generations worth of dust, and wondered what had been going on in Lucy Chalmers mind to let this go.

Morag popped out from behind the stairs, "Come along."

He followed her back to the servant's stairs down to the basement.

"What's with the dog?"

"I'm not sure how, but Dante found me."

"Found you?"

"Yes. What did you say the date was?"

"I didn't, December 17 2066."

She stopped abruptly, "December 17 2066."

He narrowly avoided walking into her.

She crossed a landing so small it was barely a corner and dropped down into the servants sitting room.

"What's so important about the date?"

"Hush, I'm thinking."

She waited until someone set a full cup of tea down, then picked it up and drained it.

"I can see why people thought the house was haunted. *Is* haunted."

She turned to look at him, "today's a total eclipse isn't it?"

"I don't know," he pulled out his phone to check, but the screen was blank, "out of battery."

"Probably not," she took a sip from someone else's cup.

"There was an eclipse the day I went back in time."

Zoo backed up and sat down. The person who'd been sitting on the chair sat up abruptly and backed away from it, "travelled in time?"

"Yes. Your two Morags are the same person.

"So there was an eclipse when I got here, an eclipse when I... phase shifted—"

"Phase shifted?"

"I don't know how else to explain it. I didn't die, and I didn't travel in time, I just kind of went invisible... Ah... Like a Star Trek cloaking device."

"Star Trek?"

"What? No Star Trek in your time?"

"No. I mean yes. It's just... Surreal."

Morag snorted, "aren't you supposed to be the great paranormal investigator?"

"How would you know that?"

Morag laughed, "are you dense? Your car is parked by the gate."

"Ah. Right. So eclipse for time travel and shifting."

"Right. Plus an eclipse when Dante found me," she stopped to scratch the dog's head, "and now an eclipse when you found me."

"So it's all about eclipses. How did you figure that out?"

"I did some research before I came back, only I didn't know I would get caught out. The weather conditions may have something to do with it. I can't research much further as I don't have the right kind of resources here."

"Can't you travel back to 2020?"

"I don't exactly know how I got here, but it seems I can't go back. At least, not until the conditions are right."

Zoo started to panic, "but where does that leave me?"

He looked into Morag's sympathetic gaze, "I don't know.

"But an eclipse lasts about five hours," she glanced at her watch, "if you're back in the same place, you might make it."

"*Might* make it? Shouldn't we get back up there?"

"If you like, I just wanted a cup of tea while I explained this."

He stood up and walked back to the stairs, turning to look at her as he reached the first step.

"Don't be such a wet week," she said "according to your reckoning I've been stuck here for 153 years and you don't see me complaining."

He turned back as she gulped someone else's tea, "how have you survived?"

She stood up, "I believe that *technically*, this is still my wedding day. So more to the point, what are you doing here gate crashing my big day?"

He preceded her up the stairs, "doesn't *The Ghost Detectors* car give it away?"

"Of course. We're a haunted house, she gave a lopsided smile, "it had somewhat of a reputation for that in 2020. That's why they had so much trouble getting a housekeeper. I suppose my disappearance made it impossible to get another."

She paused on the ground floor, "oh yeah, what about Henry?"

"He disappeared in 1922."

After a moment she started climbing again, "then, did he send me here to start this or to stop this?" she wondered.

"I'm sorry?"

"I met Henry in 2020, and he said everything started in 1904. He sent me back to stop it, but I've been thinking maybe he sent me back to start it."

"That's a bit stalkerish isn't it?"

"Well, it now seems my Henry came from 1922, and things were a bit different then.

"Though I have to admit I'd be creeped out if I hadn't just married him. Now that I have, it's more of a chicken and egg scenario. Did I send him forward, or did he send me back?"

Zoo tried to imagine where it started, "if you and the eclipse set up a time loop, when did it start?"

"And when does it end?"

"And how does it work?"

They went back into the Drawing Room. She looked up at the ceiling, then gestured at the floor, "about here I think."

He lay down, "there must be something more than the weather. The eclipse... say a low-pressure trough, and... lightning?"

As if on cue, a clap of thunder sounded overhead.

It went dark as the building shook more dust into the air.

"Yeah," Brian said from above him, "are you hurt, is anything broken?"

"Brian?"

The dust started settling, and Zoo could see Brian, Steve and Josh's heads looking through the hole in the floor above him.

"Careful," Zoo said again, "the floor isn't safe."

The heads disappeared, followed by footsteps on the stairs.

Steve got there first, "are you okay?" he asked, ever professional, still filming.

"Where's Morag?"

"Sorry?"

"Where's Morag?" he asked again as Brian and Josh arrived.

"There's no Morag, it's just us," said Brian. "Jeez mate, how hard did you hit your head?"

"But I met her, she said it was the eclipse."

He tried to get up, but Josh put a hand on his chest to hold him down, "Don't try to get up. I've called an ambulance."

Zoo struggled, "but Morag—"

"Don't try to talk either, you fell pretty heavily, you've probably got concussion."

"How long was I unconscious?"

"Don't be daft," said Brian, "you've only just fallen."

"But I met Morag, and she said it was the day she got married, and it was the eclipse."

"You couldn't possibly have done all that in the 30 seconds you might have been unconscious."

Zoo looked at Steve, camera still recording.

How desperate did he want to look on camera?

"Time dilation," he said, hoping that if Morag wasn't a figment of his imagination, she would hear. "Was it gravity, and not low pressure?"

He turned the camera off, and his crew did likewise.

The ambulance arrived, assessed the situation and secured a brace around his neck.

They asked the team to help with the stretcher, and about that time he blacked out for a moment.

As they wheeled the stretcher out, he looked up and saw a brightly lit Master suite window.

A woman leaned out and waved at him.

"Steve, the window," he said.

"What?" Steve craned his neck, "there's nothing there."

Zoo looked back as far as he could, to see what he could see.

Not her anymore, but definitely a lit window.

Did he have the ability to see paranormal phenomenon for real now?

As the ambulance crew wheeled the stretcher through the overgrown garden, he saw children laughing and playing, running through the trees.

Were they dead? Or had they been brought here by some unknown agency?

As he was loaded into the ambulance, he saw that it was full of people.

He did not need any one tell they were dead.

He screamed.

THE END

ABOUT THE AUTHOR

Alexandria Blaelock writes stories, some of them for *Ellery Queen's Mystery Magazine* and *Pulphouse Fiction Magazine*. She's also written four self-help books applying business techniques to personal matters like getting dressed, cleaning house, and feeding your friends.

As a recovering Project Manager, she's probably too fond of sticking to plan. She lives in a forest because she enjoys birdsong, the scent of gum leaves and the sun on her face. When not telecommuting to parallel universes from her Melbourne based imagination, she watches K-dramas, talks to animals, and drinks Campari. At the same time.

Discover more at www.alexandriablaelock.com.

BOOKS BY
ALEXANDRIA BLAELOCK

SHORT STORY COLLECTIONS

The Histories of Hayward Hall
Lovelorn, Lovestruck and Love at First Sight
Common or Garden Variety Heroes
Case Files of the Wilkinson Detective Agency
Unavoidable Fates

OTHER FICTION

That Love Nonsense

MS BLAELOCK'S BOOKS

Stress Free Dinner Parties
Signature Wardrobe Planning
Holistic Personal Finance
Minimally Viable Housekeeping
Planning a Life Worth Living

SELECTED SHORT STORIES

Alma's Grace
Balancing the Book
Carmelita Basingstoke
Fate in Your Hands
Kiss of Death
Lady of the Looking Glass
Life in the Security Directorate
Long Weekend in the Snow
Love in the Past Tense
Love in the Security Directorate
Morning Star, Evening Star, Superstar
Needy Bitch
Payton's Run
Phoenix Child
Secret Singer
Shining Star
Ship in a Bottle
Simone Says Hands in the Air
Special Relativity in Space
The Bygone Boyfriend
The Day the Schedule Broke
The Ghost Detectors
The Guardian's Vigil
The Mince Pie Mystery
The Mystery of the Master Suite
The Pseudonym's Bride
The Shadow Thieves
The Time-Space Paradox
Toy Soldiers